Max and the Missing Megastar

A Cat Called Max

Max and the Missing Megastar

Terrance Dicks

Illustrated by Toni Goffe

Piccadilly Press · London

Phototypeset by Goodfellow & Egan, Cambridge
Printed and bound by Hartnolls Limited, Bodmin, Cornwall.
for the publishers, Piccadilly Press Ltd.,
5 Castle Road, London NW1 8PR

A catalogue record for this book is available
from the British Library

ISBN 1–85340–103–X

Terrance Dicks lives in North London with his wife and three sons. He has
written numerous children's books, including the following series for
Piccadilly Press: *Jonathan's Ghost*, *The MacMagics* and *The Adventures of David
& Goliath*. He has also written two informational humour books, *Europe
United* and *A Riot of Writers*, both published by Piccadilly Press.

Toni Goffe lives in Hampshire. He has been writing and illustrating
for many years.

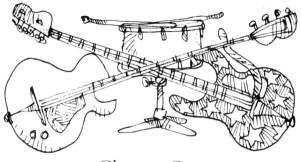

Chapter One

A Big Day for the Tigers

'WAM-BOP-A-LOOBOP-WAM-BAM-BOOM!' Timmy Tompkins' rock group – known as Timmy and the Tigers – finished the number with a medley of crashing guitar chords, and a drum roll that rattled the windows.

They all looked anxiously at the big cat in the armchair. It was a handsome, aristocratic-looking creature, all black except for white paws, a white tip to its tail, and a white patch under its chin.

'What do you reckon, Max?' asked Timmy.

Max stroked his whiskers. 'We-e-e-ll . . .' he drawled. 'Satisfactory! Indeed, positively accomplished. But remember – balance! Olly, those drums are drowning the bass guitar. Timmy, the vocals still need to come up a bit. All the elements have to blend – Rock and Roll's not just a matter of making a very loud noise, you know.'

'It isn't?' said a voice from the doorway. It was Mr Tompkins, Timmy's father. He was clutching a crumpled newspaper, his hair was standing on end and he was quivering all over. 'How can I enjoy a quiet Saturday morning breakfast – with the cup rattling in the saucer and the egg jumping up and down in the egg-cup?'

'Come on, Dad,' pleaded Timmy. 'It's

our big day!'

Timmy and his rock group had entered a national talent competition – and, with some helpful coaching from Max, they'd actually won! Their prize was an appearance on television, as part of a fund-raising charity telethon. What's more, they'd be appearing with the Diggers, the world's leading pop group.

'Don't worry, Mr Tompkins,' said Max. 'That was the last rehearsal. We'll be off as soon as the car comes. It'll all be worthwhile when Timmy's a millionaire rock star!'

Mrs Tompkins appeared carrying Samantha, Timmy's baby sister. 'The car's here, from the TV people.'

'Right, come on you lot,' said Timmy. The Tigers – Timmy, lead guitar and vocals, Tom, second guitar, David, bass guitar and Olly, drums – filed out of the house, clutching their instruments, or in Olly's case his drumsticks.

A scruffy-looking minicab was parked outside the house, with an equally scruffy young man leaning against it. 'Cab for Tompkins?'

'Car for Tompkins, and group and manager,' said Timmy. 'This old crate won't do!'

The young man shrugged. 'It's all there is. You coming or not?'

'We'll never fit in, not with the instruments as well.'

'Oh, I think we'll manage,' drawled Max. He began purring, a deep throaty purr, and his eyes glowed green . . .

Minicab and driver blurred for a moment – and suddenly, in their place, stood a long, gleaming black limousine, a smartly-uniformed chauffeur standing beside it. He saluted and opened the door

and Timmy and the others climbed
inside. The driver closed the door and got
behind the wheel, Timmy waved
goodbye to his astonished family, and the
limousine glided away.

It was amazingly comfortable and
roomy inside the limousine. Max touched
a button and a well-stocked mini-bar
appeared. 'Refreshments, anyone?
Lemonade, a cola?'

They sat back sipping their cokes and soon the streets of London glided by on the other side of the smoked-glass windows. In an incredibly short time they were drawing up outside a huge circular building. 'We're here!' said Timmy excitedly. 'It's the Television Centre.'

A huge uniformed commissionaire was guarding the outer gate. He saluted and the barrier rose. 'Use the VIP car park, driver.' The car slid smoothly up the drive and parked just in front of the building. Another commissionaire, even bigger than the one on the gate, sprang forward to open the door.

Timmy nodded towards the limousine. 'Shouldn't you . . .?'

'Ah yes,' said Max. His eyes glowed green. There was a sort of spangling sound, and suddenly a scruffy minicab stood in the VIP car park.

The outraged commissionaire roared
'Oy, you! Get that old heap out of here!'

As the confused minicab driver
roared away, Max turned to the
commissionaire. 'Now, we need Studio
One, if you'd be so kind?'

'This way, sah!' The commissionaire
led them along curving corridors through
a set of double doors and into Studio One.

Like any television studio, it was a huge

barn-like room with rows of lights in the ceiling, and lots of space for the cameras. Studio One had been turned into a concert hall for the occasion. There was a central stage with a set of drums and some amps, surrounded by cameras and lights.

There was a little group of musicians on the stage, a drummer, a guitarist and a bass guitarist. They were talking in low voices with a tubby little man in earphones.

'That's the Diggers, there on the stage!' whispered Tom. 'Look, Bozo, Al, Mo.'

'That's only three out of four,' said David. 'Where's Stevie? He's the real star!'

Suddenly Bozo shouted, 'Look, it's no use yelling at us, Arthur, me old mate. I've no idea where Stevie Digger's got to. He's evaporated! Vanished! He's totally disappeared!'

Chapter Two

A Megastar is Missing!

Timmy went up to the little man. 'Er,
excuse me, I think we're supposed to
report here. Timmy Tompkins and the
Tigers.'

'What?' The little man stared wildly at
him. 'Sorry, I'm a bit upset. I'm Arthur
Upshaw, floor manager.' He checked his
clipboard. 'Timmy Tompkins, that's
right. And you're all here?' Timmy
waved round the little group. 'Me, Olly,
Tom and David. Max here is our

manager.'

'Do I gather there's some kind of a crisis?' asked Max.

'You might say that,' said Arthur bitterly. 'We've only lost the lead singer of the most famous rock group in the country.'

'Really? And how did you manage to do that?' asked Max.

Bozo, the Diggers' long-haired drummer, said grumpily, 'Look, we'd just arrived and we went off to the

canteen, right?'

Al, the tall skinny guitarist, took up the story. 'After a cup of your legendary coffee, Stevie decides to stretch his legs.'

'But he doesn't come back,' said Mo, the massive bass guitar player. 'So after a bit, Al goes off to look for him.'

'I checked the ring road, that little garden and everywhere,' said Al. 'I went right round the building. Not a trace.'

'Then we all joined in,' said Bozo. 'Nothing! We thought he must have come back here.'

'Which he certainly hadn't!' said Arthur.

Max stroked his whiskers thoughtfully. 'Could he have left the Centre? Got distracted, changed his mind about doing the show?'

'There's no record of him at any of the gates,' said Arthur.

'And as for him just wandering off, forget it,' said Al. 'Stevie never missed a show in his life.'

'He must be meaning to come back,' said Bozo. 'Look, he left his favourite guitar here.' Max picked up the guitar and studied it thoughtfully.

'He left his book as well,' said Mo, holding out a luridly-covered paperback. It was called *Professor Why and the Zardoks,* and the cover showed an oddly-dressed man grappling with hideous mechanical monsters.

Max put down the guitar, took the paperback and said 'Hmm . . .'

'It's from the science-fiction show,' said Bozo. 'Stevie's a real fan.' He looked round. 'Well, let's hope he's all right. At least he was still wearing his lucky yellow sweater.'

All this time more people had been

drifting into the studio. By now there was a very large lady in a silk gown, a juggler, a conjuror in full evening dress, and a troupe of performing dogs all yapping loudly.

'Well, the show must go on,' said Arthur. 'We're way behind on the rehearsal schedule already. All right, Tigers, you're next.'

A little overawed by playing before a world-famous group – well, three-quarters of it – Timmy and the others did their number. When it was over everyone clapped, including the three Diggers. 'We'll have to watch our step,' said Al cheerfully. 'Pretty soon you'll be chasing us up the charts!'

The large lady came on stage and started singing an operatic aria in a very loud voice. 'I bet she can shatter glass with her high notes,' whispered Timmy.

'She's shattering my ear-drums,' said Max. 'We cats have very sensitive hearing. I think I'll take a look around.'

'Not without me, you won't,' said Timmy. The rest of the Tigers were happily watching the rehearsal and chatting to the Diggers. There was a little canteen in the corridor outside the studio.

'Let's try a cup of the famous TV Centre coffee,' said Max. A jolly lady in a green overall sold them two plastic beakers of murky brown fluid, and they carried them over to a Formica-topped table.

'Come on, Max,' said Timmy. 'You're up to something!'

'I thought I might look into this mysterious disappearance.'

'Good idea. I'll help.'

'What about your performance?'

'You saw that lot in the studio. It'll take ages to rehearse all them. As long as I'm back for the show . . . Where do we start?'

'We've started,' said Max. 'We're re-creating the crime.' He tasted his coffee and shuddered. 'And speaking of crimes . . .' Max put down his cup. 'Now then, Timmy, imagine you're our missing megastar, after some fresh air. Which way would you go?'

Timmy looked up and down the corridor. Just off to the right a glowing

sign read EXIT. 'That way I
suppose . . .'

They walked along the corridor and
went through the door. They found
themselves on a road, which ran right
round the Centre.

'Which way would *you* choose for a
walk?' asked Max.

Timmy looked up and down the road.
To the left was a clutter of trolleys piled
high with bits of scenery. To the right the

road was clear, with a glimpse of grass
and trees. 'That way!' They set off to the
right, and soon came to the entrance to a
sizeable garden.

'That's the "Gardening Time" garden,'
said Timmy. 'They do programmes from
there every week. I wonder if he went in
there?' They went into the garden and
looked around. There were gravel
paths, ornamental trees and bushes,
a greenhouse, a pond with a little

fountain . . . At the end of the garden a stretch of smooth green lawn sloped down to a dense hedge.

Timmy wandered down to the edge of the lawn. 'Max, look!' The smooth turf was all churned up by heavy foot-marks, and there was one long mark leading towards the bushes. 'It's as if someone was dragged across the lawn,' said Timmy excitedly. Hot on the trail, he followed the drag-mark into the bushes. 'The hedge has been pushed aside, Max. You can see by these broken twigs . . .'

With Max close behind him, Timmy forced his way through the hedge to a wall with iron railings on top. Jumping up, Timmy grabbed the railings and pulled himself up. Max sprang up beside him. On the other side of the wall was a quiet back-street.

'We're right on the edge of the Centre,'

said Max thoughtfully. Timmy nodded. 'Well, it's pretty obvious what happened. Stevie came into the garden and someone jumped out of the bushes and grabbed him. They dragged him back here and heaved him over the wall. They must have had a car waiting . . . Hey, look at this!' There was a strand of yellow wool, snagged on the railings.

'It's from Stevie's lucky yellow sweater,' said Timmy. 'Well, that clinches it – Stevie's been kidnapped! But who did it?'

Timmy jumped down and started searching around in the bushes. After a few minutes something black and gleaming caught his eye. He grabbed it and straightened up. 'Max, look at this!' Timmy held up his find. It was a black leather gauntlet, covered with metal studs. At the end of the fingers gleamed claw-like metal tips. 'Do you know who wears gloves like this?'

Max studied the gauntlet with distaste. 'I have no idea.'

'Kongo, that's who! Kongo the Monster of Rock!'

Chapter Three

The Monster of Rock

Max just looked baffled. 'Who, dear boy?'

Timmy said, 'Surely you've heard of Kongo and the Killers?'

Max shook his head. 'Enlighten me!'

'Well, they're this really evil heavy metal band . . .'

'What do they do that's evil?' drawled Max. 'Play out of tune?'

Timmy grinned. 'They play so loud it'd be hard to tell! They dress up in weird, scary costumes. Their whole act is

21

weird, lots of smoke and bangs and flashes, mock sacrifices, buckets of fake blood splashing about . . .'

'Not really my idea of entertainment,' said Max.

'Kongo and Stevie are rivals – it's a legendary show business feud,' Timmy went on. 'Stevie's into all the good causes, fund-raising for famines and refugees, anti-racism and anti-sexism, save the ozone layer and the whale. Kongo's always making fun of him, calling him Mr Clean.'

'I take it Kongo doesn't support all these good causes?'

'Kongo only supports *bad* causes. His songs are always getting banned . . . Don't you see, Max, it's just got to be Kongo!' Timmy turned and headed out of the little garden. 'Come on, Max!'

Max jumped down from the wall and

followed him. 'Steady on, old fellow!
Come on where?'

'Kongo lives all alone in this big house
in a village called Elmwood, just outside
London. We've got to get down there,
rescue Stevie, and get him back here in
time for the concert!'

'Shouldn't we tell the police about what
we've found and get them to make some
enquiries?'

Timmy was jumping up and down

with impatience. 'Max, please! That could take forever. It's only a few hours till the concert – we've got to get Stevie back right now!'

'Oh very well,' said Max. 'I suppose we'd better look into it.'

Timmy stared at him, rather hurt by the lack of enthusiasm. 'What's the matter, Max?'

'I'm not really sure, my dear chap . . . But there's something . . .' There was a rapidly-approaching roaring sound. 'How fortunate,' said Max. 'We need some transport – and here it comes!'

A leather-clad, helmeted courier zoomed past them on a massive motor-bike. Max stared after the rapidly retreating machine. His eyes glowed green and he purred deeply. Suddenly the motor-bike simply stopped. Then it began to move backwards, coming towards them. A few moments later it was pulling up beside them. The burly, leather-jacketed courier said feebly, ''Ere . . .'

Max stared at him with hypnotically glowing green eyes. 'I'm afraid we've got to commandeer your splendid machine, old chap. Vital mission for the good of the Television Service. Just let's have that jacket, will you? And the helmet, of course.' Dazedly, the courier got down from his machine and propped it upright. He took off his jacket and helmet. Max passed them to Timmy who put them on. The jacket was so big it served as a sort of overcoat. Surprisingly, the helmet fitted better.

'What about you, Max?'

Max climbed onto the saddle. 'I've got my own kind of protection, but you humans have to be careful. Get on behind

me and hold on!' Timmy scrambled on to
the bike behind Max, clasping him tightly
around his middle. Max kick-started the
bike and they shot away. They roared
along the ring road and soon came to the
main gate. The barrier was down and an
agitated commissionaire was waving to
them to stop.

Timmy could hear the clanging of an
alarm bell. He shouted in Max's ear. 'That
courier must have made a quick recovery
and reported a stolen bike!'

'Pity!' yelled Max. 'No time to explain now. Hold tight, Timmy!' Max twisted the throttle and heaved back on the handlebars. The motorbike soared up into the air like a champion show-jumper, cleared the barrier with ease, landed neatly on the road outside and zoomed away.

For Timmy the journey passed in a blur. They sped up a ramp and bombed along the motorway. They left the motorway for a minor road, turned off into a country lane and came to a sudden stop. Max said, 'Timmy, I think we've arrived!'

Timmy pulled off the helmet and sat blinking in the sunshine. They were outside the gates of a big old country house. Even in daylight, its twisted turrets and crooked chimneys made it look like Dracula's Castle. The big iron gates were firmly closed and a notice read: 'Private! Keep Out! Ferocious Guard Dogs! Man Traps! Mines! Trespassers Will Be Shot! This Means You!'

'This is the place all right!' said Timmy. He looked uneasily at the big gate with its rows of spikes. 'I suppose we're just going to fly over that as well?'

'Let's do things the easy way for once, shall we?' There was a black box fastened to one of the stone pillars of the gates. Max stared hard at it, his eyes glowed green, the box vibrated and whirred . . . The gates swung open and Max and Timmy rode inside. The gates closed behind them. Max got off the bike and Timmy did the same. 'Softly, softly, I think', said Max, propping the bike up against a tree. 'We shall proceed on foot.'

'What about the dogs and the mines and the man traps?'

'We'll cope with those when we come to them,' said Max. 'Trust me, dear boy!'

They set off up the path which led them into a thicket of dense shrubbery. Timmy crept cautiously after Max, expecting the growl of a guard dog, the bang of a mine or the clang of a man trap at any minute. But nothing happened. They emerged into a clearing where a big fair-haired young man in blue overalls was working on a colourful flower bed. He looked up. 'Hullo, who are you?'

'Couriers from the Television Centre,' said Max. 'We have an urgent message for Mr Kongo.'

'All right. Give it to me and I'll see he gets it. I'm his gardener, caretaker and general dogsbody.'

'We have to deliver the message in person,' said Timmy.

The young man looked worried. 'That could be a bit tricky. Kongo hates strangers – and he gets very nasty when he's upset.'

'You mean he gets violent?' asked Timmy.

The young man nodded. 'Dreadful! Some fans climbed the fence last week. They were lucky to get out alive!'

'I'm afraid we must insist on seeing him,' said Max.

'Well, if you want to risk it, it's your neck. Just follow the path up to the house, don't try any short cuts, it's not safe. When you get to the house, ring the bell. I can't guarantee he'll let you in – and you'll probably be safer if he doesn't!'

'Thank you,' said Max and set off up the path.

Timmy hung back for a moment. 'How do you stand it, working for someone like Kongo?'

'Oh he's not so bad,' said the young man. 'It's just this savage temper of his. He's always sorry afterwards, when he bashes someone. Pays all their medical expenses while they're in hospital . . .'

'Thanks,' said Timmy. 'That makes me feel much better!' He hurried after Max.

The long winding path brought them up to the main house at last. They climbed the stone steps to a metal-studded

door. There was a pull–bell beside it.
Timmy looked at Max. 'You're sure you
want to do this?'

'My dear fellow, it was all your idea!'

'Right!' said Timmy grimly. He
grabbed the bell and pulled. A deep
clanging came from somewhere inside the
house. Nothing happened, and Timmy
heaved on the bell again. The clanging
came again. Suddenly the door creaked
open. Timmy and Max went inside, and
the door slammed behind them. They
found themselves in a dark and gloomy

hallway. Just ahead was a set of double doors, slightly ajar.

Timmy looked up at Max who said, 'After you, dear boy.' Timmy gulped and made his way through the doors, Max at his heels. They were standing in a huge, cavernous hall, with a stage at the far end.

Suddenly there was a flash of light, a loud thunderclap and a cloud of smoke. When the smoke cleared, a tall, terrifying figure stood on the stage. It was dressed in metal studded black leather, and it wore huge high-heeled boots. Beneath piled-high jet-black hair the face was a ghastly white.

'Who comes to disturb Kongo, the Monster of Rock?' roared the terrifying apparition. 'Depart or die!'

Chapter Four

The Monster's Lair

Suddenly Timmy noticed something. On its left hand, the figure wore a metal-clawed gauntlet. But the right hand was bare. Timmy's hand went to the gauntlet in his pocket.

'Prepare to die!' screamed Kongo. Thunder rolled and lightning flashed. Instinctively, Timmy shrunk back – but Max didn't seem to be bothered at all.

'Very impressive,' he purred. 'As it happens, I've a trick of my own I'd like to show you.'

His eyes glowed green and he purred louder. The terrifying figure of Kongo rose up in the air – and started spinning like a Catherine wheel. As it whirled round, bits of costume started flying away from it. A black gauntlet, a black wig, high-heeled boots, leather jerkin and trousers . . . Slowly the figure stopped spinning and dropped to the stage. Timmy looked at it in astonishment. Wearing only a pair of baggy boxer shorts, still with his white make-up on, there stood the friendly caretaker they'd met on the way in.

'You!' said Timmy. 'You're Kongo!'

'That's right,' said Kongo. He looked admiringly at Max. 'That's some special effect! I could use you in my stage show!'

Timmy waved at the black leather gear scattered around the stage. 'But why . . .?'

Kongo shrugged. 'Just protecting my privacy.' He fished some jeans and a T-shirt from a corner of the stage and started putting them on. 'I happen to be a peaceful sort of bloke, who enjoys a quiet life. Bit of gardening, bit of fishing . . .' He began to scrub the make-up off. 'But the fans won't leave me alone. I have to find ways to keep 'em away.'

'Hence all the horrifying notices,' murmured Max.

'Exactly. They're all bluff . . . There isn't a guard dog, a mine or a man trap on the place. The wall and the gate and the notices put most of them off. If anyone does get past the gate, I do my caretaker act and spin 'em a few horror stories. And if that doesn't work I dress up in the gear and scare them off myself.'

'Well, maybe you are nice and ordinary

underneath,' said Timmy sternly. 'But it still doesn't explain this!' With a flourish, he produced the other black gauntlet.

'Hey, where did you get that?' asked Kongo. 'I lost it at a big gig. Thought a fan must have pinched it.'

'You lost it at the TV Centre when you kidnapped Stevie Digger!'

Kongo stared at him. 'Me? Why would I do a thing like that?'

'To stop him appearing on the Charity Telethon. I expect you hoped they'd ask you to take his place.'

'You're crazy! Stevie's a mate – and I've already turned down the Telethon anyway.'

'Oh yes?' said Timmy scornfully. 'It's easy enough to say that.'

Kongo went over to a desk on the other side of the room, rummaged through some papers and produced a letter which he thrust at Timmy. 'Take a look!'

Timmy studied the letter which was on Television Centre writing paper. 'Dear Mr Kongo,' he read. 'I'm sorry you feel you can't appear on our Telethon, but I quite understand that "doing good" doesn't fit with your public image! We've followed your suggestion and asked Mr Stevie Digger, and I'm happy to say he has agreed to appear. P.S. Many thanks for your extremely generous donation of . . .'

The figure which followed had so many noughts on the end it made Timmy blink. He passed the letter to Max. 'It could be a forgery . . .'

Max studied the letter. 'I'm afraid not, Timmy. The paper's quite genuine, and that's certainly the Director-General's signature.'

He passed the letter back to Kongo. 'It only remains for us to apologise and withdraw.' Max led the way out, pausing for a moment in the doorway. 'Oh, just one more thing . . . the er, gig, where you lost the gauntlet. Was anyone else appearing with you?'

'Only Stevie and the Diggers. We had a chat about the Telethon in the interval. All that feud stuff's just for publicity.'

Max nodded. 'With two such eminent

performers appearing – I assume there were all the usual security arrangements?'

'Guards everywhere,' confirmed Kongo. 'Someone got away with my gauntlet, though. Cunning devils, these fans.'

'They are indeed,' said Max. 'Well, our renewed apologies, Mr Kongo. Come along, Timmy!'

Very soon they were on the big motorbike again, zooming back along the road to the TV Centre. When they arrived, Max handed over the bike to a bemused commissionaire. 'Just see to this, will you, there's a good chap!'

They went up the steps into the reception area. 'Now what?' asked Timmy. 'It'll be time for the Telethon soon, we still haven't found Stevie, and my case has collapsed!'

'It was always a bit too good to be true, don't you think, dear boy?' drawled Max. 'The signs of struggle and the gauntlet were deliberately planted to put suspicion on Kongo – and to lead us away from the real criminal.'

'And who's that then?' asked Timmy. 'Admit it, Max, you don't know who kidnapped Stevie or where he is now any more than I do!'

'Oh, I think I do, dear boy,' said Max calmly. 'I've known for some little time . . .'

Chapter Five

The Enemy Within

Timmy stared at him. 'You what?'

'I've a pretty good idea about the who –
and the where. That book Stevie left
behind, *Professor Why and the Zardoks* . . .
The science-fiction show it's based on is
recorded here?'

Timmy shrugged. 'I imagine so.'

Max went over to the reception desk.
The smartly dressed young lady who sat
behind it said, 'Can I help you?'

'You can indeed! I wonder if any

"Professor Why" recordings are taking place today.'

'I'm afraid that information is confidential, sir.'

'Oh well, I'll just have to ask my friend the Director-General.'

With a sudden helpful smile the young lady said, 'I'm sure there's no need for that, sir. I'll check for you.'

As she looked through some lists, Timmy whispered, 'Sometimes name-dropping works even better than magic!'

The receptionist looked up. 'I'm afraid "Professor Why" recordings finished last week. But there's a special effects test listed for this evening, in the workshop in B Block.'

Max turned to Timmy. 'Go back to Studio One and bring *all* the Diggers to the special effects workshop. Hurry!'

Timmy hurried away. Pounding along

the curved corridors he arrived breathless
on the floor of Studio One, where an
agitated conference was taking place
between the three Diggers and Arthur the
studio manager.

'Well, if he doesn't turn up, we'll just
go on without him,' Bozo was saying. 'Al
can do lead guitar and vocals, and the rest
of us will just have to play a bit louder!'

Timmy ran up to them. 'Max wants
you all to come to the special effects

workshop – now! It's urgent! It's about Stevie.'

'This way!' said Arthur. He led them along corridors until they reached B Block, a low building set a little apart from the main centre. Timmy pushed open the heavy double doors and they went inside. The room was in semi-darkness except for an illuminated area at the far end. There stood one of the hideous metal creatures so well known to every TV viewer – a Zardok! It gleamed evilly under the spotlight.

There were three shadowy figures just inside the door – and one of them was Max. 'Ah, there you all are,' he said. He indicated a bearded bespectacled man. 'Allow me to introduce the producer of "Professor Why" . . .' Max turned to a small, keen-faced man in a white lab-coat. 'And this is the special effects designer.

Now, allow me to explain the situation. Our hero, the Professor, escaping from his deadly enemies the Zardoks, chances upon the empty shell of a Zardok awaiting repair, and hides inside. Unfortunately a group of Tharg Resistance Men, fighting the Zardok invasion of their planet, happen to come along. Seeing only one of their deadly enemies, they blow it up!'

'I want a really spectacular blow-up,' said the producer.

The special effects designer said, 'This is our first test. We've put strips of plastic explosive all round the edges of the Zardok. They'll be set off electrically when I press that button.' He nodded to a control desk in the corner.

'Right,' said Max. 'Fire away!'

Suddenly Al, the Digger's second guitarist, screamed, 'No! No!'

'Take no notice,' said Max. 'He's a bit over-excited. Carry on!' Max moved in front of Al, blocking his way, preventing his frantic attempt to get to the special effects man who was moving to the control desk. 'Press the button, old chap!' called Max.

'No, please, don't!' yelled Al. 'You mustn't! You'll kill him!' It was too late. There was a flash of light, an amazingly loud bang and the Zardok went up in

flame and smoke.

'You've killed him!' shouted Al. 'You've killed Stevie – and it's all my fault. Stevie was inside that Zardok!'

'How do you know?' asked Max sternly.

'Because I put him in there. I didn't want to harm him, just hide him. And now he's dead!'

'No, I'm not, Al,' said another voice. A tall, beaky-nosed young man in a yellow sweater appeared from a dark corner.

'Stevie!' shrieked Al – and fainted . . .

'Pure jealousy, I'm afraid,' said Max. 'Poor Al couldn't bear always being number two. He thought if the Diggers could only perform just once with him in the lead he'd be the star!'

'But what happened?' asked Timmy.

'How did he do it?'

It was some time later. First-aid men had carried the unconscious Al away and they were all back in Studio One.

'I imagine he caught up with Stevie on his walk,' said Max. 'Then he suggested they pop into the special effects workshop to see the Zardok. He knew Stevie was a big fan of the show.'

'That's right,' said Stevie. 'When we got there he lifted the lid of the Zardok so I could look inside. That's the last thing I remember. Everything went black, and I woke up inside the Zardok. He'd jammed the lid somehow so I couldn't get out.'

'Then he went back to the garden and faked those kidnap signs,' said Timmy. 'Including dropping Kongo's gauntlet which he'd pinched earlier at the concert. How did you know it was him, Max?'

'I didn't at first,' said Max. 'Though that gauntlet always did seem a bit too good to be true. It wasn't till we were on our way back from Kongo's that I realised that if Al was telling the truth he'd have seen all those kidnap signs himself when he checked the garden after Stevie vanished.'

'But they weren't there till he made them himself – hoping someone would soon spot them and blame Kongo. Some twit like me!'

'A perfectly natural mistake, dear boy,' said Max. 'Anyway, by the time I arrived at the workshop, the producer and the special effects chappie were wondering why mysterious thumps and muffled cries were coming from a supposedly empty Zardok. We fished Stevie out – but it struck me it might be revealing to blow up the Zardok, with Al thinking Stevie was still inside.'

Timmy looked at Stevie. 'Are you going to tell the police?'

Stevie shook his head. 'I reckon poor old Al's been punished enough. Still, he won't be up to playing tonight – which leaves the Diggers short of a guitarist. How about it, Max?' He handed Max Al's guitar. 'It's all ready to go . . .'

'My dear fellow, I couldn't possibly,' protested Max. 'Mind you, I used to strum a bit, once upon a time . . .'

Slinging the guitar-strap casually over his shoulder, Max suddenly produced a superb rippling guitar-riff that echoed round the studio. Heads turned and everyone cheered . . .

The Telethon was a huge success, raising lots of money for charity. Timmy Tompkins and the Tigers were a big success too. But the unexpected hit of the evening was the grand finale. A spectacular guitar duel between Stevie of the Diggers and his surprise guest guitarist – the Magnificent Musical Max!